For my father

R.H.

For Jim and Jenny

H.L.

ORCHARD BOOKS
338 Euston Road, London NW1 3BH
Orchard Books Australia
Level 17/207 Kent Street, Sydney, NSW 2000

ISBN 978 1 84362 590 2

First published in 2006 by Orchard Books
First published in paperback in 2007

Text © Richard Hamilton 2006
Illustrations © Helen Lanzrein 2006

A CIP catalogue record for this book is
available from the British Library.

1 3 5 7 9 10 8 6 4 2

Printed in Singapore

Orchard Books is a division of Hachette Children's Books

This Orchard
book belongs to

_____

_____

_____

THE
SECRET
CAVE

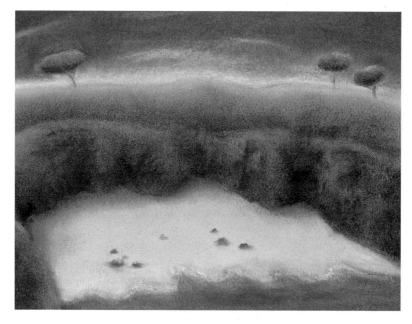

RICHARD HAMILTON
ILLUSTRATED BY HELEN LANZREIN

ORCHARD BOOKS

High on a cliff,
above the shining sea,
Johnny found a path that led
through tall grass
and butterflies
and heather.
He held Dad's hand as they
clambered down together.

"Dad!" cried Johnny. "Look! A beach."
Between the cliffs
the beach lay silent, secret, still.

Johnny ran –

    across warm stones,

      over crackling seaweed;

down to the sea,

    down to the waves

      washing onto the sand.

And then, by the rocks,

   he saw a cave –

      hidden, dark, mysterious.

Who once lived there?

Who lived there now?

The dark, damp sea smell

   made him wonder . . .

Did pirates bury treasure here,

then board their ship and sail away?

Or, on dark nights in wintertime,

was this where smugglers   hid casks of wine?

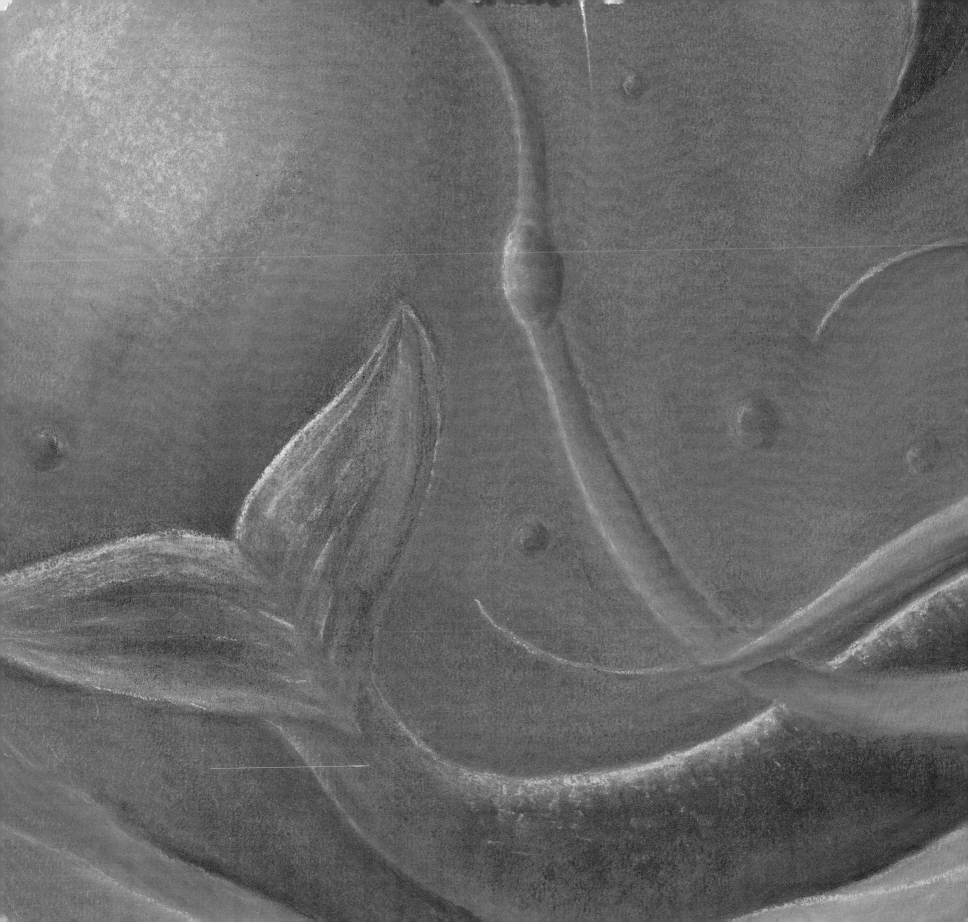

Did this cave lead to Neptune's watery world,

where mermaids swam, with scaly tails and seaweed hair,

singing songs to sailors?

Or, was there a sea-dragon in the dark,
that ventured out when feeling brave?

"What a fantastic cave!" cried Dad.

"Shall we go in?"

Johnny held Dad's hand tightly.

His heart thumping,

feet scrunching on the pebbles.

Deeper and deeper

into the cave they went . . .

But they found no pirate treasure.

No wine.

No sea-dragon.

No mermaids with seaweed hair.

Just rock.

Ancient, centuries-old, solid rock.

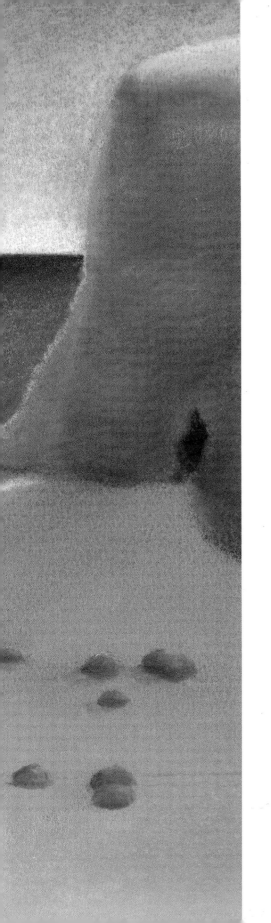

And suddenly Johnny ran.

He ran back into the sunshine,
onto the wide open beach,
beside the vast blue ocean,
under the endless sky.

They had their picnic there,

    watching birds swoop over the swelling sea.

Afterwards they searched for shells,

    and peered into rock pools,

        and drew figures in the sand.

Until they climbed back together –

through tall grass

and butterflies

and heather.

And that night, Johnny snuggled

under the covers

in his own warm cave.

He fell asleep with the sound of the sea

singing in his ears;

dreaming of the day

he and Dad found their secret cave.